**Please check all items for damages
before leaving the Library.
Thereafter you will be held
responsible for all injuries
to items beyond reasonable wear.**

Helen M. Plum Memorial Library

Lombard, Illinois

A daily fine will be charged for
overdue materials.

MAY   2015

DESERT DANGER

J. BURCHETT & S. VOGLER

STONE ARCH BOOKS
a capstone imprint

Wild Rescue books are published by Stone Arch Books
A Capstone Imprint
1710 Roe Crest Drive
North Mankato, Minnesota 56003
www.capstonepub.com

First published by Stripes Publishing Ltd.
1 The Coda Centre
189 Munster Road
London SW6 6AW
© Jan Burchett and Sara Vogler, 2012
Interior art © Diane Le Feyer of Cartoon Saloon, 2012

Cataloging-in-Publication Data is available at the Library of Congress website.

ISBN: 978-1-4342-3773-6 (library binding)

Summary: A lion cub has fallen down a well, and now its mother is preventing
the locals from getting any water! Ben and Zoe travel to the Kalahari desert
to help, but with overwhelming heat, deadly creatures at every turn, and a
powerful sandstorm raging around them, Ben and Zoe will have to dig deep to
set things right.

Cover Art: Sam Kennedy
Graphic Designer: Russell Griesmer
Production Specialist: Michelle Biedscheid

Design Credits: Shutterstock 51686107 (p. 4-5),
Shutterstock 51614464 (back cover, p.148-149, 150, 152)

Printed in the United States of America in Stevens Point, Wisconsin.
032013   007240R

TABLE OF CONTENTS

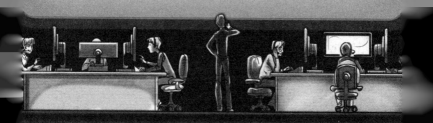

WILD RESCUE

MISSION

BEN WOODWARD
WILD Operative

ZOE WOODWARD
WILD Operative

BRIEFING

TARGET:

CODE NAME: JOSSY

CHAPTER 1

A HEATED RACE

Zoe turned her go-kart and accelerated down the brightly lit race track. "Woohoo!" she yelled, pulling farther away from Ben.

There was no way Ben could catch up to his twin sister now. There was one more lap to go. Zoe would win this race for sure.

Just then, someone flagged Zoe down. "The track must be closing early," Zoe said to herself. She maneuvered off the raceway and braked hard. She came to a stop a few feet from the woman with the flag.

Zoe was just taking off her crash helmet when Ben came screeching to a halt right behind her. He watched as Zoe ran over to the woman, recognizing her immediately.

"Erika!" Zoe cried out in excitement. She looked around to make sure that no one else was within earshot. "Do we have a new mission? Is that why you're here?"

"Yes," said Erika. "I'm here to take you straight to your destination."

Ben and Zoe were by far the youngest operatives in WILD, a top-secret rescue organization run by their uncle, Stephen Fisher. Erika Bohn was his second-in-command. Whenever WILD received news of an animal in danger, Erika showed up suddenly, wherever Ben and Zoe were. Before they knew it, they'd be heading out for another WILD rescue mission.

Erika grinned. "Sorry I interrupted your race," she said.

"No problem, Erika," Ben said, grinning widely. "We'll just call this last race a draw."

"No we won't!" said Zoe. "I was in the lead the entire —"

Zoe was cut off by a revving go-kart engine. Before she could speak, Ben zoomed away to return his go-kart.

Zoe rolled her eyes. "Boys," she said.

* * *

A few moments later, they were all driving down the highway in Erika's car toward a private airfield. Ben quickly sent a text message to their grandma, letting her know that they wouldn't be home tonight.

Grandma took care of Ben and Zoe while their parents were working abroad as vets. She knew all about WILD, and was very proud of her brave grandchildren.

Zoe watched from the front seat as they passed the white, barren fields. Evergreen trees were lit briefly in the car's headlights as they passed. "I wonder what kind of animal we'll be helping this time," she said.

"You know the drill," said Erika. "In the glove compartment, you'll find a clue from your uncle."

Zoe reached into the compartment and pulled out a glass eyeball. Using a penlight she found inside, she inspected the eyeball. It had an orange and brown iris with a round, black pupil.

"It reflects the light," she said, turning it in the beam. "So it's probably a copy of a nocturnal animal's eye."

Ben reached over from the back. Zoe gave him the eye and the penlight. "And it's big," he said. "I bet it's from a member of one of the wild cat species."

"I agree," said Zoe. "Let's see what Uncle Stephen has to say."

Ben gave her the eyeball. Zoe carefully placed it into a slot in the vehicle's dashboard. Immediately, a small hologram of a man appeared in front of them. He wore a white lab coat and had a hat sitting on top of his messy hair.

"Greetings, my nephew and niece!" said Uncle Stephen. "Your destination for this mission is Africa."

"It's definitely not a tiger, then," said Ben.

"Africa is a king-sized clue to the animal you'll be rescuing," Uncle Stephen's hologram said. "Call me as soon as you've figured out the answer."

The hologram disappeared.

"A king-sized clue," repeated Zoe. "That has to mean —"

"The king of the beasts!" interrupted Ben. "Wow! We're rescuing a lion. That'll be exciting!" His eyes went wide. "And a little scary."

"Your BUGs are under your seats," Erika told them. "Go ahead and give your uncle a call with your answer."

Ben and Zoe never went on a mission without their BUGs — the Brilliant Undercover Gizmos their uncle had invented. They looked like handheld video games, but had lots of wonderful applications, like satellite maps, communicators, and animal tracking devices. Zoe took her BUG, hit the call key for WILD HQ and turned on the speakerphone.

"Good evening, Ben and Zoe!" came their uncle's voice. "Did you figure it out yet?"

"Yep," said Zoe. "It's a lion!"

"Well done," said Uncle Stephen. "You're headed to the Kalahari Desert in Namibia."

"Awesome!" said Ben. "So what's the mission this time, Uncle Stephen?"

"Here at HQ, we picked up a news report on a Namibian radio station," Uncle Stephen said. "A lioness has been seen prowling around a local well for a few days. That well is the only source of clean water for the locals, and they won't dare go near it because of the angry lioness."

"Lionesses don't usually live alone, do they?" asked Zoe.

"I don't think this one is alone," said Uncle Stephen. "There have been several reports of strange sounds coming up from the bottom of the well."

"Did one of the lioness's cubs fall down the well?" Ben asked.

"That's the most likely explanation, yes," said Uncle Stephen. "It's probably calling out for its mother."

Erika drove the car through an open gate toward a rough track. "That would also explain why the lioness won't leave the area," she added.

"Oh, that poor cub," said Zoe.

"Don't worry, sis," Ben said. "We're going to rescue it!"

"And return it to its mother as soon as possible," said Uncle Stephen.

Uncle Stephen's voice grew serious. "Otherwise, the cub will soon starve to death," he said. "We don't know how long it's been down the well, or if it's injured. That's why we're flying you straight there."

"We need to preserve as many Namibian lions as we can — especially the young ones," Erika said. "Their numbers have been declining recently due to disease — and because of humans, unfortunately. People illegally hunt lions, and there have been several cases where lions were poisoned for being too close to farms."

"You should land in Namibia in the morning — local time," Uncle Stephen said. "Your equipment's already been loaded onto the WILD Jet. There'll be plenty of time on the journey for you to watch the desert training videos."

"We learned about sandstorms in the climate chamber last time we were at WILD HQ," Ben said, reminding their uncle.

"And that will come in very handy," said Uncle Stephen. "But you also need to be able to survive ordinary desert conditions. The Kalahari is a dangerous place, so I'm glad you won't be out there very long. Good luck. Over and out."

Erika stopped the car next to a small plane idling on an airstrip. "You'll be taking a vet's kit with you in case the cub needs attention," she said as they jumped out of the car. "And tranquilizer guns, of course."

Ben nodded. "Good," he said. "We don't want the lioness eating us while we're rescuing her cub!"

"How about ropes to climb down the well?" asked Zoe.

Erika nodded. "You know it," she said. She swung open the door of the plane so the twins could climb aboard. "Inside, there's also lightweight clothing that reflects the sun to help keep you cool. It's summer out there — and extremely hot."

"What's our new gadget, Erika?" asked Ben. "Uncle Stephen always comes up with something new and amazing for our missions."

Erika strapped herself into her seat. "Your uncle's really excited about this one," she said, adjusting several knobs on the jet's console. "But you can't see it until we get to Namibia."

"Then what are we waiting for?" said Zoe. "Let's fly!"

CHAPTER 2

THE WASP

"Wow!" Zoe said as she jumped down from the WILD Jet. She and Ben gazed all around them. Small bushes and plants pushed up through the red sandy soil of the Kalahari Desert. In the distance, smooth dunes rose up and down in hills and valleys. The morning sun was just peeping over the horizon. It cast long shadows over the entire desert.

Ben put on the goggles that he found in his backpack. The tinted lenses curved around his face for a perfect fit.

"These are pretty cool," Ben said, striking a pose.

Zoe rolled her eyes. "Yeah, they're cool all right," she said. "But you definitely aren't!"

Erika chuckled as she climbed down from the cockpit. "They're sun and sand goggles," she said. "They'll protect your eyes during sandstorms. Your uncle also gave them a zoom function, so you won't need binoculars." She pointed at the middle of the device. "There's also a built-in light to help you see the cub in the well."

"Wow," Ben said. "Uncle Stephen's really outdone himself this time."

Erika smiled. "These aren't your new gadgets," she said. "You'll see your new toy in a second. Anyway, how does the desert clothing fit?"

"Perfectly," said Zoe. She did a little twirl in her lightweight shirt and pants. "And very comfortable."

Ben groaned. "Nice moves, twinkle toes," he said. Zoe stuck her tongue out at him.

"Can we see our new gadget now?" Ben asked.

"Yes," said Erika. She walked to the rear of the plane. "I'd like to have landed closer to the well, but this is the nearest strip of land that's clear of rocks. You have a few miles to travel, so you'll be using a WASP."

Ben and Zoe exchanged confused glances.

Erika smiled and pulled a lever. A hatch slowly opened. A ramp slid down until it was resting on the sand. Erika disappeared into the dark cargo hold for a moment.

When Erika appeared again, she was dragging something covered in a tarp down the ramp.

"This is the WASP," said Erika. She pulled back the cover with a dramatic yank. "Also known as the Wind- and Solar-powered Pod."

The twins gazed at the sleek, boat-shaped vehicle in front of them. It had a light frame with two seats, a small motor at the back, a gear-shifter, and a steering wheel.

"A dune buggy!" said Ben. "I've always wanted to try one of these."

"This is no ordinary dune buggy," said Erika. She reached into the frame of the vehicle and raised a telescopic mast. A shiny, silver sail extended from it. "This works the same way as a sail on a boat. The sail also acts as a solar panel. Even when it's folded to the mast, it absorbs enough light to charge the engine's battery. So even when there's no wind, you won't be stuck without power."

"It's awesome," said Zoe.

Ben inspected the controls. "How fast does it go?" he asked. "After all, we might need to outrun a lion. They can sprint at speeds of 35 miles per hour over short distances, you know."

Zoe rolled her eyes. Erika laughed. "Dr. Fisher told me to warn you to take it easy with them, Ben," she said. "He designed the WASP to get you to your destination — not to race lionesses."

Ben grinned. "I'm just glad it's not another camel." He grimaced, remembering a painful ride in Africa. "I should be able to stay on this thing."

Erika loaded their backpacks onto the buggies. "I hope there's lots of food in those," said Ben.

"Do you ever stop thinking about food?" asked Zoe.

"There's the usual rations," Erika said. "There's also a special powdered formula for the cub in case the mother isn't able to feed him right away."

"Did you know lions drink their mothers' milk until they're around six months old?" Ben said.

Zoe sighed. "Thank you, Mr. Know-it-all," she said. "But they do start eating meat in addition to mother's milk a while before that point."

"You'll just need to add water to the bottle for the cub's milk," said Erika. "There's a water tank under the WASP's frame. Remember to drink plenty yourselves. It's very easy to get dehydrated out here."

"I can't wait to get going," Ben said.

"Good!" said Erika. "I'm off to a wildlife park in Botswana now. There's been an outbreak of blue tongue disease in the deer and antelope, and your uncle has developed a new, faster-acting vaccine. I'm delivering the first batch."

"I've heard Mom and Dad talking about blue tongue disease," said Zoe. "It can be fatal."

Ben nodded. "And if the deer and the antelope die out, that means there will be less prey for predators like lions."

"Speaking of predators, we can't forget our scent dispersers," said Zoe. She scrolled through her BUG menu and activated her disperser. "We don't want any lions to think we're meals-on-wheels."

Ben chuckled. "Agreed," he said.

Ben activated his scent disperser and jumped into the WASP's driving seat. "Hop in, Zoe!" he called.

"Wait a sec," said Zoe. "I was the champion go-kart driver. I should drive."

Ben grinned. "If I remember correctly," he said, "our last race ended in a tie!"

Zoe chuckled. "Yeah, keep telling yourself that," she said.

"Make sure to keep your tranquilizer guns on you at all times," said Erika, interrupting them.

Zoe nodded and climbed in next to her brother. "Don't worry, we will," she said.

Zoe called up the satellite map on her BUG. She pointed to distant sand dunes just beyond a clump of trees with gnarled trunks.

"It looks like we have to go east to get to the well," Zoe said.

"Then we'll need to use the engine," said Ben. "There's not much wind here."

Zoe pulled down the sail, then Ben flicked a switch. The motor whirred gently to life.

"Bye, Erika!" said Zoe. "We'll contact you the minute we get the cub back to its mother." Zoe turned to her brother. "Take it slow and steady, Ben."

Ben grinned. "I know what I'm doing," he said.

CHAPTER 3

DESERTED

As soon as Erika climbed into the plane,
Ben slammed his foot into the accelerator.
The WASP skidded across the bumpy earth,
swerved from side to side, then stopped
with a sudden jolt.

Ben looked at his sister's shocked face
and burst out laughing. "Just kidding," he
said with a grin. "You should see your face,
though!"

Zoe playfully socked Ben in the arm.
"Jerk," she said.

Ben accelerated again, this time steering the vehicle slowly and expertly between the small boulders that littered the hard, red earth. Already the temperature was rising. Zoe and Ben pulled on their hats with flaps that covered their necks.

"Look!" Zoe said. "There's something moving over there."

Zoe set her glasses to full zoom.

"Hyenas," Zoe said. "There's no mistaking the way they hunch their backs. We should stay away from them."

Ben nodded. He steered the WASP around a group of scraggly brown trees that were topped with small yellow leaves. "Check those out!" he said. "I read about them on the plane. They're elephant's trunk plants."

Ben wove between low plants and sparse patches of grass.

"This is a very strange place," said Zoe. "There's more vegetation than I expected."

The sun rose in the sky. A light breeze blew up. "Time to raise the sails!" said Ben.

"Don't worry," Zoe said. "The expert's here to handle it."

Ben gave her a mocking salute. "Aye, aye, Captain!" he said.

Ben brought the WASP to a stop and flicked a switch to turn off the engine. Zoe climbed into the driver's seat and released the sail. It billowed out and caught the wind immediately. Soon the WASP was sailing from side to side across the sand.

"Awesome!" yelled Zoe. "It's almost as fun as real sailing."

"Better than real sailing!" Ben yelled back. He checked the map, holding tightly to his BUG as they jolted along. "We're almost there. Just another mile or so."

"There's a hollow up ahead," said Zoe, peering out over the shimmering landscape. "And I can hear goats."

"We'd better check it out," said Ben. "There could be people looking after their herds down there. If so, we'll have to change our route so they don't see us."

"Agreed," said Zoe. "Two children traveling on their own out here? They'd definitely try to stop us. They wouldn't know we're on a vital mission or that we have the skills to survive here."

"And we couldn't tell them," said Ben. Zoe nodded.

Zoe let the sail flap loose as Ben braked. The buggy came to rest behind a clump of thorny bushes.

They climbed out and crept across the hot sand to where the land dipped away. Using the bushes and grass as cover, they were able to glance down at a herd of goats in the valley below. They were grazing while being watched over by two small figures.

"They're just kids," said Ben. "Let's go talk to them."

"Do you think we should?" Zoe asked. "After all, we don't want to attract attention to ourselves."

"Maybe they know something useful," said Ben. "They probably know about the well we're looking for. They might even be able to tell us if the lioness is still there."

"Then we'll have to put translators in so we can understand everything they say," said Zoe. She peeled off the small rubber earpiece from the side of her BUG and popped it into her ear.

Zoe scrolled through the menu of her BUG. "I looked it up on the plane," she said. "They speak a form of click language called Nama, although many Namibians speak English too." They both found Nama and entered it into the translator.

"All right, let's go," Ben said. They slipped their BUGs into their pockets and walked toward the grazing herd. The two children stood together. One was a girl a little younger than Ben and Zoe. Her hair was tightly woven into braids, and she wore a bright red T-shirt over a wraparound skirt.

The other goatherd was a boy who seemed to be around five years old. The girl held a long spear in her graceful hand.

"Hello!" Ben called as he and Zoe approached. The goatherds looked up and stared at them.

"Can you help us?" Zoe asked slowly. "We are visitors in your country."

The two goatherds glanced at each other but didn't speak.

"We've traveled a long ways," said Ben. "We are thirsty." He clutched his throat and stuck out his tongue. "Water!"

The girl took a jar that was bound in cowhide from her belt. Without a word, she handed it to Ben.

"Thank you," he said, taking a small sip.

Then he handed it to Zoe who did the same. Asking for a drink was a good excuse to talk to the two kids, but Ben and Zoe didn't want to leave them short of water in this hot, dry landscape. Ben dug through his backpack and pulled out two of Uncle Stephen's special energy bars. He passed them to the girl, who inspected them.

"Cherry," she read slowly.

"You speak English?" said Zoe.

The girl nodded. "A little," she said. "But my brother doesn't." She handed a bar to the little boy, who unwrapped it quickly and began to eat.

The boy turned to his sister. "I like it," he said in his own language. Ben and Zoe had to pretend they didn't understand.

The boy smiled brightly at them,
nodding his head and rubbing his tummy.

Ben and Zoe smiled and grinned back.
"I'm Ben," Ben said. "This is my sister,
Zoe."

"My name is Tukwenethi," said the girl.
She waved a hand toward her brother.
"And this is Jossy."

"Thank you for the water," said Zoe, handing back the bottle. "Is it from a well or a pool?" she added. Ben smiled. *That was a clever way for Zoe to ask for information about the well,* he thought. *They won't suspect anything.*

"All our water is from wells," said Tukwenethi. She pointed to the north. "There is a pool there, but it is bad water. It makes people sick. Only animals drink from it."

"Is your well far away?" asked Ben.

"Not far," Tukwenethi said. "About two hours' walk. But we cannot use it. There is a lion mother there and she will not let us get near. Now we have to go to the next well. It is a day's walk away."

Jossy pulled at his sister's arm. In their language, she told him what she had said.

Jossy's eyes widened. "There's a ghost in the well!" he said. His translated words rang in Ben and Zoe's earpieces. "It moans and cries out. Mommy said someone went there last night and it was still there. I would be brave and fight a lioness, but not a ghost."

Ben gave Zoe a knowing glance. The cub was alive!

Jossy spun around and stared up at the far side of the hollow. Now Ben and Zoe could hear something too. Adult voices, speaking in Nama. And they seemed to be coming closer.

Ben and Zoe looked at each other in alarm. They had to disappear — and quickly!

CHAPTER 4

THE DARK DESCENT

Tukwenethi turned to see where the voices were coming from, shading her eyes from the glare of the sun.

"We have to leave," whispered Ben. "If we go back the way we came, we can hide behind the bushes."

"But the two goatherds will see us leave," Zoe whispered back.

"I'll make sure they forget about us for a moment," Ben said. He scrolled through the menu on his BUG.

Ben pointed his BUG toward the herd. At once, the hologram of a cheetah appeared in the middle of them. The terrified creatures skittered about, bleating in fear.

Spear raised, Tukwenethi and her brother ran to see what was wrong.

"Done," whispered Ben. He shut off the hologram before the two goatherds could see it. "Let's go!"

Ben and Zoe scrambled up the side of the valley and hid behind a bush. They watched as two men hurried down to see why the goats were so agitated. The moment the children couldn't see them anymore, they darted back to the WASP.

"I feel bad about not saying goodbye to Tukwenethi and Jossy," said Zoe. "But we have to continue our mission."

Zoe pulled the sail until it caught the wind. Ben released the brake, and they were once again sailing across the sand.

Ben checked the satellite map on his BUG. "The well is just a short distance away," he said.

"We'll finish this mission before lunchtime!" Zoe said cheerfully.

"Now who's obsessed with food?" Ben teased.

They continued to glide across the desert, their WASP soaring over the dunes. The bushes were less common now, and the ground was sandier. The ground shimmered in the heat of the morning sun.

Zoe adjusted the WASP's course to catch the breeze. "The well should be near here," she said.

Ben checked his tranquilizer gun. "As soon as we're in range of the mother, slow down and I'll put her to sleep," he said. "We'll give her the smallest dose we can so she'll wake up quickly. That way, she'll find her cub once we've rescued it."

"There's the well," said Zoe. "It's up ahead."

The dusty, open ground led to a small stone mound with a simple wooden framework and pulley above it. A rope trailed down into the well.

"I can't see the lioness, though," said Ben, looking all around. "Where is she?"

"Probably left to hunt for some food," whispered Zoe. "We're going to have to be careful. She could come back at any moment."

They let the WASP roll slowly along the track toward the well while checking for any signs of movement. When the WASP came to a halt, they jumped out, folded up the sail, and grabbed their tranquilizer gun.

Zoe watched as Ben took a rope from the back of the buggy and ran over to the well.

Every rustle of leaves in the bushes made Zoe whirl around and grip the tranquilizer gun tightly. She felt her heartbeat thunder in her ears.

"I hope nothing's happened to the cub since last night," she whispered anxiously. "It could have fallen into the water and drowned."

Ben activated the spotlight on his glasses and peered down into the well's narrow circle of darkness.

"I can't see anything yet," Ben said, shining the light across the black expanse. "Wait a minute. Did you just hear something?"

Zoe tensed. She heard a barely audible wailing sound echo up from the depths of the well.

"The cub's still alive!" Zoe said in relief. "But it doesn't sound like an animal at all. I'm not surprised the local people thought the well was haunted."

Ben inspected the pulley above the wooden framework. "That might be strong enough to hold a bucket, but not one of us," he said. "But we can tie the rope to the WASP and wedge it against the well."

"You climb down the well and I'll keep watch," Zoe said. "But hurry."

Ben brought the WASP over to the stone wall and tied the rope to the frame of the vehicle.

Zoe suddenly raised the tranquilizer gun. "Freeze!" she whispered. "The lioness is back."

With their breaths held, Zoe and Ben watched as a large animal emerged from behind a rock. She had a long, sleek body. Her powerful muscles shifted under her golden coat as she moved. Her tail swished as she padded purposefully toward the well.

"Can you hit her with a dart from here?" Ben whispered between clenched teeth.

Zoe shook her head. "No," she said. "I'll try to get to her side."

The big cat stopped as she caught sight of Ben. The lioness let out a low, deep-throated growl. Zoe's finger tightened around the trigger as she edged away from the well.

But the creature suddenly crouched, ready to pounce. Zoe had to shoot!

POP! As the dart struck the lioness's side, the terrified animal snarled and whipped around to see what had attacked her.

The next second she was bounding toward Zoe. She backed away. For one long, terrible moment it looked like the dart had not effected the beast.

But then the lioness's steps faltered. Dragging herself up on to the stones of the well, the lioness slumped down. Her head hung drowsily over the well's rim.

Slowly, Ben crept up next to her. She was completely unconscious now. He felt a stab of panic at being so close to this deadly predator.

"She was trying to protect her baby," whispered Zoe. "If only she knew that we're here to help." She gently stroked the lioness's ear. "We'll soon have your little one out of there."

"We need to hurry," said Ben. "We don't have long."

Zoe sat on the WASP, gathered up the loose rope, and held it tightly. "I'll feed out the rope as you descend," she said.

"And then just hit reverse on the WASP to pull me back up," said Ben. "I'll give two tugs when I'm ready."

Ben took the free end of the rope and tied it around his legs and waist, making a harness. He eased his legs over the edge of the well and found a foothold. He gave Zoe a thumbs-up to let more of the rope out. Then he began to squeeze past the warm, limp lioness. At that moment, the sleeping animal gurgled and her lips twitched, revealing a row of huge, sharp teeth. Ben froze. Had the tranquilizer begun to wear off already?

The lioness's mouth relaxed and she went still again. Ben took a deep breath to calm himself and edged his way into the well. He searched for footholds in the rough stone. He stopped and looked down.

Far below, the water gleamed in Ben's spotlight. His stomach turned — the well was much deeper than he'd thought. He moved his head, trying to locate the cub. He couldn't see anything, so he began to climb down.

The sides of the well were slippery. Ben knew that he would have to take it slowly or he'd fall. He inched his way down, wedging his fingers into tiny crevices. Then he paused to rest. Above him was a tiny circle of sky, broken by the outline of the lioness's head. He shined his light down and caught sight of a little ledge near the bottom. The glint of two round eyes reflected back at him.

He'd found the cub!

Suddenly, the narrow sides of the well seemed to be pressing in on him.

Ben began to feel hot and panicky. He started to think that he couldn't go any further.

Then he heard a faint, pitiful mew. Forgetting his fears, Ben climbed down toward the sound.

The cub was lying on the ledge. By light, Ben could see its golden fur, the dark spots on its head, and every rib sticking out of its body. It raised its head weakly as Ben dropped into the narrow space next to it.

"We're going to get you back to your mom," Ben said to the little creature.

He slowly reached out, grabbed the cat by the scruff of its neck, and held it tightly in one arm. The cub barely struggled.

Ben tugged the rope twice to give the signal. At once, he heard the distant whir of the WASP engine echoing down the stone walls. The rope tightened as he felt himself being hauled up toward the warm light.

At last he could feel the warmth of the sun on his head and shoulders. He was about to reach for the edge of the well to haul himself up when he realized he was level with the face of the lioness. The bleary eyes were flickering open.

The huge creature was awake — and staring right at him!

CHAPTER 5

JOSSY

Ben could feel the cub struggling weakly in his arms as it smelled its mother's familiar scent. Any second now, she would realize her baby was there. If Ben moved, the lioness would attack.

Zoe watched, horrified, as the lioness stirred. She couldn't leave the buggy. Without her weight holding it in position, Ben and the cub would fall back down the well.

The rumbling in the animal's throat

grew louder and more threatening. Then the lioness got to her feet and turned to face Zoe! There was only one thing to do. She had to tranquilize the mother again. Zoe raised the gun and fired. The lioness stumbled, turned, and fell to the ground.

Ben hauled himself and the cub over the edge of the well. As soon as the rope went slack, Zoe jumped off the WASP and ran over to help him.

"Are you okay?" she asked. "You're shaking."

Ben laid the little cub gently on the ground. "I thought she was going to eat you," he said nervously.

"No way," Zoe said with a grin. "She didn't stand a chance against my super-quick trigger finger."

Zoe gazed at the baby lion. "You are a beautiful little boy, aren't you?" she said. She stroked the soft fur of its big, floppy paws. "But it looks like you could use a good meal. Let's check you out and see if you're okay."

They both knelt beside the cub. "He doesn't look too bad, considering the poor thing fell pretty far down the well," said Zoe, checking the cub's limbs.

"The ledge was near the water, so he's been able to get a drink, at least," Ben said. He set the cub on his feet. The little creature tried to take a step but collapsed.

"Is he too weak to walk?" asked Zoe, lifting him up. "Wait, what's this?"

A deep gash ran down the inside of the cub's left front leg. He mewed and struggled weakly as Ben inspected the wound.

"The wound is bad," he said. "This little fella needs treatment."

"Then we have to help him," said Zoe. "There's no way we can leave him with his mom. They'll never get back to their pride. They'll be sitting targets for any predators around. And this cut could get infected."

Ben nodded. "Looks like our mission has changed," he said. "We need to fix his leg."

"And take him back to his family ourselves," said Zoe. "That is, if we can find his pride." She glanced around at the dry, dusty desert as it baked in the intense heat. "This was supposed to be the end of our mission. Now we don't know how long we'll be out in the Kalahari."

"We'll be okay," said Ben. "We have the kit, the WASP, and plenty of food and water." He stroked the soft fur under the young lion's chin. Ben stood. "We'll let WILD know about our change of plans, but first let's get out of range of our friend over there." He jerked a thumb toward the sleeping lioness. "I don't want to be around when she wakes up and smells her son. There's not enough wind to make a fast getaway, so I'll drive."

"Fine with me," said Zoe. "That means I get to hold this little fella!" She picked up the cub and climbed onto the WASP. She made the cub comfortable on her lap. "I'm going to call you Jossy — after that nice boy we met earlier." She stroked his soft fur. "I'm sorry we have to take you away from your mom for a little while, but it's for your own good."

Ben jumped in and turned on the engine. "I say we head for the pool that Tukwenethi told us about. She said all the animals go there. So I bet that Jossy's pride drinks at it, too."

"I'll find it on the BUG," said Zoe. She held it above the dozing cub and began to scroll through for the satellite map. "That's where his mom will probably go when she wakes up and realizes her baby is gone. But hopefully not until we're far away."

"Then we'll have to make sure she doesn't catch up to us," said Ben.

"It took you forever to get down the well and back," said Zoe. "And she only woke up when you were almost out. So she should be asleep about the same amount of time again." Then a thought hit her. "The lioness won't know we've taken her cub, Ben. She might stay at the well!"

"Good point," said Ben. "We'll have to leave her a trail to follow." He reached over the side of the WASP and picked up a handful of stones. "If we rub these against Jossy's scent glands and drop them as we ride, hopefully she will pick up the scent and come after her cub."

"But that basically makes us bait," warned Zoe. "We'd better get a lot of distance between us and her."

"No problem," said Ben. He reversed the WASP away from the well.

"You need to head northwest," said Zoe, pointing. She navigated through her BUG menu. "I'm going to fire a tracking dart into our lioness first. That way, we can keep an eye on her location."

"Good idea!" Ben said. He circled the WASP around the well as Zoe aimed the BUG at the lioness. As soon as the little dart had been fired, Ben turned the wheel and hit the accelerator, and they zoomed away.

An orange light pulsed next to the well on Zoe's screen. "Poor lioness," she murmured. "I've made her into a pincushion with all my shots."

"She'll be fine," Ben said. "Just remember, it's for their own good."

Zoe smiled warmly at Ben. She nuzzled her finger under the sleepy cub's chin.

* * *

They traveled onward. Every now and then, Zoe rubbed a stone against Jossy's cheek and dropped it over the side. She checked the tracking signal. "Mom hasn't woken up yet," she said.

"Then I think it's safe to stop and fix Jossy's leg," said Ben. The WASP came to a halt by the thick trunk of a baobab tree. Its fan-like branches cast a small shade in the hot midday sun.

"It'll be nice to escape the heat for a while," Zoe said.

Ben mixed Uncle Stephen's special powdered formula with water and tried to feed it to the cub.

"He should be really hungry, but he's hardly taking any," Zoe said.

"Maybe his leg's hurting him," said Ben.

Zoe checked the wound. "I'm not a vet," she said, "but it looks too deep to ignore."

"Let's ask Uncle Stephen what to do,"
said Ben. "We need to tell him what's
happened so far, anyway."

Ben took his BUG and hit the call key for
WILD HQ.

"Hello!" came their uncle's voice. "Have
you reunited the little cub with his mom
yet?"

Ben told him about their mission
changing. "Quick thinking, you two,"
said Uncle Stephen. "But don't forget that
leaving a scent trail can attract all sorts
of predators. You'll need to keep your
eyes peeled at all times. I'll let Erika know
you've been delayed. You can contact her
when you're ready for a ride home."

"Before you go, we need some advice,"
Zoe called into the speaker. "We think the
cub's cut needs stitches."

Ben held the BUG over the deep cut, took a photo, and sent it to Uncle Stephen.

"Looks rather nasty," said their uncle. "But you can glue that together."

Ben and Zoe gave each other confused looks. Then Zoe slapped her forehead. "Of course!" she said. "Medical glue for wounds. Mom showed me once on a horse that had a cut on its flank."

Ben searched through the vet kit and pulled out a small tube of ointment. "Wound-bond," he read.

"That's it," said Uncle Stephen. "Wash the cut, then close the wound with the bonding agent. Then give the little fella a dose of antibiotics. Over and out — oh, and make sure you don't glue your fingers together. It's powerful stuff!"

Zoe chuckled. "Bye, Uncle," she said.

After filling a syringe with water and antiseptic, Ben squirted the wound until he was sure that it was clean. Then he applied the glue. Zoe carefully squeezed the cut's edges together.

Jossy barely moved.

"That's amazing!" exclaimed Zoe. "It's stuck shut already. It's like super glue." She scratched the little cub gently between the ears as Ben gave him an antibiotic injection. "You'll be back on your feet in no time, Jossy."

Ben looked out over the surrounding desert. "We should get going," he said. "We don't want his mom to catch up."

Zoe nodded. "I'll keep checking her signal as we go," she said.

Soon the WASP was bumping along over the rough terrain. The sun was high in the sky now. The dunes stretched away to their right, a brilliant red in the glaring sunlight. Zoe rubbed another pebble on Jossy's fur and threw it behind them.

Ben wiped his forehead. "It's so hot. Like being in an oven," he said, taking a swig from his water bottle.

Zoe peered through her goggles, adjusting the zoom. "It's so hot there are hardly any animals around," she said. "There are some giraffes way over there. I see a flock of birds hovering above the trees in the south."

"I suppose most creatures are waiting for it to cool down a bit," said Ben.

Zoe gasped suddenly. "Something's following us," she said.

Zoe adjusted her goggles to zoom in on the view behind them, focusing on the bare land they'd just traveled over and frowned. "I can't see it now," she said, "but I swear there was an animal on our trail."

Ben grinned as he steered the WASP around a clump of elephant's trunk plants. "You're just nervous," he said. "Or the heat's playing tricks on your eyes."

"I hope so," said Zoe, keeping watch over her shoulder. She peered into the distance. "No, I was right. Something's definitely tracking us."

Ben brought the WASP to a halt and turned. The air shimmered with heat, but in the distance he could see the movement of a large animal. The creature was getting steadily nearer.

"Can you tell what it is?" Ben asked.

"It's all so hazy that's it's hard to see," said Zoe. "Some sort of big cat, I think." She checked the BUG screen. The orange light pulsed in the same place as before. "It's not Jossy's mom — she's still by the well."

Zoe refocused her goggles. Her eyes went wide behind the lenses. "I can see a dark mane, Ben," she said, her voice shaking. "It's a lion . . . and it's big."

Ben let out a low whistle. "He's big all right," he said. "And he looks like he's in rough shape and hasn't eaten in a while. That only makes him more dangerous."

"Let's get moving and hope he doesn't see us," said Zoe urgently. "Hopefully our scent dispersers will do their job."

Ben stiffened. "He's raised his nose!" he said. "He may not be able to smell us, but I think he's following Jossy's scent." Ben hit the accelerator. "Our little friend here would make a good meal for a hungry lion," he said. "And we'd be his dessert!"

Zoe looked back anxiously as the WASP accelerated. The lion was bounding toward them, closing the gap with every step. "Will the WASP be fast enough to outrun it?" Zoe asked.

Ben floored the accelerator. "We're about to find out," he said.

CHAPTER 6

A WILD CHASE

The WASP zoomed across the desert. The lion was galloping now, sand flying as his pads hit the ground. He was outpacing the WASP. It would only be a matter of time before he caught up to them.

"Tranquilize him!" Ben yelled to Zoe. "It's our only hope."

"I can't!" Zoe yelled. She held the cub tight. "Jossy will fall if I let go of him."

They hit a small rock, sending a jolt through the WASP. Jossy yelped in pain.

Zoe risked a look back. The cub's cry had spurred the lion on. "Faster!" she screamed. "He's catching up to us!"

"We're going as fast as we can," Ben said through clenched teeth.

He could see the start of the sand dunes rising up ahead. His heart sank. That would slow them down even more — and maybe the lion, too.

Then the WASP hit the slopes. As it struggled to climb the sloping sand, Ben leaned forward, urging the machine up the hill.

"The lion!" screamed Zoe.

Ben glanced over his shoulder. The creature was in pouncing distance. He could see his sharp teeth as his lip curled into a snarl.

As they reached the top of the hill, the lion leaped. His claws scraped across the back of the WASP. At that moment, they surged over the peak and began to accelerate down the steep slope, sand flying behind them.

Zoe twisted in her seat. The lion was panting hard and trying in vain to stay on his feet. Laying in the sand, the creature looked scrawny and old.

"You did it," Zoe cried. "We outran him!"

"I'm not slowing down yet," Ben yelled back.

They zoomed down the dune and up the next, hurtling to the bottom at high speed.

"Watch out!" yelled Zoe.

They were heading toward a stretch of small, sharp boulders. Ben tried to swing the WASP around to avoid them, but it was too late.

CRACK! The WASP shuddered, lurched to one side, then flipped over. "Jossy!" yelled Zoe. She climbed out of the vehicle and scrambled to her feet. "Is he okay?"

Ben got out and crouched down to examine the motionless cub. "I hope so," he said. "I saw him roll out of your arms, so he didn't fall far."

Zoe gently stroked Jossy's head. The cub made a faint mewing sound. "He looks okay," Zoe said, "but what about you?"

Ben grinned. "Just a few bruises," he said. He went to inspect the WASP. It was tipped on its side a short distance away from them.

"Let's see if we can get the WASP back on its wheels," Ben said. As he walked around the other side of the vehicle, he let out a low whistle. "One of the wheels is broken. And the axle has snapped. This isn't going anywhere."

"Then we're on foot," said Zoe, hoping she sounded calmer than she felt.

Ben looked back at the way they'd come. "We seem to have lost the lion, thankfully," he said.

"If we carry everything in your backpack," said Zoe, "we can use mine to carry Jossy. No time to hang around here. We'll update Erika after we're absolutely sure the lion's not around anymore."

"We need food and water," Ben said. He picked up Zoe's bag and began to empty it. "And the vet kit, of course."

Ben hurriedly unclipped the sail from the WASP. "This will make a good shelter," he said. He folded it up and put it in his backpack with their sleeping bags and the rope. "Everything else has to stay."

Zoe carefully placed Jossy in her backpack. Then she went to help Ben unfasten the water tank.

"In this heat, we'll need all the water we can carry in this heat," Zoe said. Then she noticed the dark wet patch on the ground beneath the WASP. She touched it with her fingers and gasped.

"Ben!" she said. "The tank's been punctured. Our water's gone!"

CHAPTER 7

JUST DESERTS

Ben gave the water tank a desperate shake. "There's a little left in the bottom," he said. "Quick, hand me a bottle."

"That's not going to last us very long," Zoe said as Ben collected the last of the water in his bottle.

"Then the sooner we get Jossy home, the better," said Ben.

He helped Zoe hoist her backpack onto her shoulders. Zoe felt Jossy's hot little breath on her neck.

"We might get thirsty," Zoe said, "but at least we've got some milk for you, Jossy."

Ben placed the flap of the pack over the cub's head to protect him from the sun. Then he fired a tagging dart into the seat of the WASP and covered the buggy with sand as much as he could.

"Erika should be able to find it when our mission's over," Ben said. "Hopefully no one else will."

Zoe checked the map on her BUG. "Escaping that lion has taken us way off course," she said. "We need to head west now, over the dunes again."

Ben looked at his watch. "It's two-thirty," he said. "We have about four hours before nightfall. Plenty of time."

"We can't leave any trails," said Zoe. "We don't want Jossy's mom catching us. That last stone was pretty far back, so she shouldn't be able to track us. We'll just have to hope she'll head to the pool."

"Check her signal," suggested Ben.

"She hasn't moved yet," said Zoe. "She must still be sleeping."

They set off toward the slope of the next dune. The hot sun beat down upon them. They could feel the heat of the earth through their boots.

The ridge of the red hill stood out sharply against the blue sky. "I researched dunes when we were in the plane," Ben said. "Very interesting stuff, although I didn't think we'd be walking over them."

"What's so interesting about piles of sand?" said Zoe.

"There's more to them than that," said Ben. "The steep slope of a dune is called the slipface. It's really hard to climb. We're lucky because we're going up the gentler side, where the sand's firmer."

"Good!" said Zoe, taking the first step on to the dune. But her leg muscles soon began to ache as she trudged up the slope.

"And the ripples are where the wind's blown the sand," Ben said.

"Thank you, Mr. Encyclopedia," said his sister. "I'll tell *you* something — the sand's so hot that my feet are burning!"

Zoe stopped to shift the straps of the heavy backpack. Jossy snorted in his sleep, right next to her ear. A spider scampered across the sand. It stopped and began to dig, burying itself so it could wait for its prey.

"I wish we could find cover like that," said Zoe.

Ben let out a little chuckle. He looked very tired.

After a long climb, they reached the high ridge. Ahead, long and smooth dunes lay in waves across the landscape.

"Amazing!" cried Zoe. "It looks like a huge red ocean." She glanced at the steep slope in front of them. "But how do we get down that?"

"Wanna race?" asked Ben, grinning.

"Don't be silly!" said Zoe. "I'd never be able to keep my balance with Jossy on my back."

"You won't have to keep your balance," Ben said. He sat down facing the steep slope. "This isn't called the slipface for nothing. It's like a slide."

Zoe sat beside him and put the backpack on her knees. "I'm ready," she said.

Ben let out a shout as they pushed off, sending sand tumbling after them as they went.

"That's the way to go!" said Zoe, shaking sand off her arms at the bottom of the slope.

"Although I didn't expect to travel across the Kalahari on my butt," she added. She stood up and groaned. "Jossy's feeling really heavy now that I'm on my feet again."

"I'll take Jossy for a while," Ben said.

They continued swapping backpacks as they made the slow climb up each dune, then slid their way down the slipface. The sun beat down relentlessly the whole time. Each slope seemed harder than the last.

Zoe flopped down onto the sand. "I don't think I can go any farther," she said. "This heat is draining my strength. We need to take a rest. And some water."

With the weight of Jossy dragging on his shoulders, Ben was feeling the strain too. "If we can make it out of the dunes, there might be some shade," he said, trying to sound cheerful. "We can have a picnic!" He held out his hand and pulled his sister to her feet.

Zoe crawled up the slope ahead, licking her dry lips.

Zoe was trying hard to drive the image of cool, fresh water from her mind. At last she reached Ben at the top. "No more dunes!" she said in relief.

They stared out over the vast stretch of flat land below. Sparse shrubs and grasses poked up from the red earth. With their goggles on full zoom, Ben and Zoe could make out the treeline in the far distance, surrounded by an area of vegetation.

"That must be the pool," said Ben.

"But I can't see any shade around here," said Zoe. Her throat felt like sandpaper. "Maybe we can use the sail as shelter."

They slid down the last slope and pulled out the sail. Draping it over their heads, they made a makeshift tent and flopped down under its welcome shade.

Ben eased his backpack off and laid it down. Jossy woke up and began to wriggle. Ben offered him some milk. The little cub drank thirstily.

Ben grinned at Zoe. "That's a good sign," he said.

"We'd better be careful so he doesn't get too lively," said Zoe. "We don't want him escaping."

Zoe drank a mouthful of water. She had to force herself not to have any more, despite wanting to drain the bottle dry. She handed it to Ben.

"We'd better update Erika," said Ben. "She might not be able to land the plane here, but maybe she could drop us some supplies."

Zoe pressed the call key on her BUG.

They waited to hear Erika's voice come out from the BUG, but nothing happened. "That's strange," said Zoe. "The screen is blank."

"Maybe yours is malfunctioning," said Ben. He tried his own BUG, then shook his head. "Mine's dead, too. Even the tracking and satellite systems aren't working. Maybe it'll start working again after we move to a different position. Maybe the dunes are affecting it."

But Zoe wasn't listening. She was staring in delight at the ground a few yards in front of them.

Ben looked up to see a group of small, skinny brown creatures with big dark eyes scurrying around. "Meerkats!" he whispered.

They watched the energetic group
sniffing and digging as they tossed up the
earth behind them. The babies tumbled
about, biting each other playfully. Two
large adults stood bolt upright on a nearby
rock. Their heads swiveled this way and
that, checking the area for any signs of
danger.

Ben looked at his sister and grinned. "Cuteness overload," he said with a groan.

"But they're so cute!" said Zoe. "Look at that little one playing with his friend's tail."

Jossy gave a loud mew and tried to climb out of the backpack. Ben laughed. "No, Jossy, you can't go and play with them!"

Suddenly, one of the lookouts gave a shrill cry. In less than a second, every last meerkat had vanished into their burrows in the ground.

"They're frightened," said Zoe, glancing around. "Did Jossy scare them away?"

Ben shaded his eyes and looked up. "Might have been an eagle," he said. "Sorry your little friends have scampered off, but at least we can get moving again."

Ben swung his backpack onto his shoulders. Jossy poked a paw out and batted at the flap of his hat.

Zoe was pointing straight ahead. "That's why the meerkats ran off," she cried.

Ben followed her finger. A swirling orange wall was eating up the land, slowly moving closer and closer. "A sandstorm," he said. "And we're right in its path."

"Remember our training in the WILD climate chamber," said Zoe. She pulled out two cotton scarves. When they'd both covered their noses and mouths, she tightened her grasp on the WASP sail. "We have to face away from the storm." The sail flapped wildly in the hot, dry wind that grew stronger every moment. As they pulled the sail over them, they felt the sand beating at the metallic fabric.

Wide awake now, Jossy wriggled out of the backpack. Ben grabbed at him with one hand, but the little cub squirmed free.

In the next instant, he disappeared into the storm.

"Jossy, no!" Zoe cried.

CHAPTER 8

SANDSTORM

Zoe dived out into the swirling storm. She felt the sand beating against her skin, stinging her like sharp needles. Bent over, she stumbled around, calling out for Jossy. But her voice was muffled by the howling wind.

He's not a trained animal, Zoe realized. *He won't come to my call, but he must be somewhere nearby. He might even have gone back to the shelter.* She turned, but couldn't see the sail any longer. She was totally lost now.

Zoe fought down her rising panic as she crawled on, trying to find something to focus on, anything that would tell her where she was. But she couldn't make out any landmarks, just endless swirling sand. She should have stayed in the shelter with Ben, but she knew she'd had no choice. She had to find Jossy.

The sand was pelting her goggles. She started to feel dizzy as she watched its swirling movement. She took an uncertain step forward, stumbled, and fell heavily. As she stretched out her hand to pick herself up, she felt her fingers come into contact with something warm and moving.

Zoe's instincts kicked in. She pulled back her hand and curled up, arms over her head, fearing an attack. She could hear something crying out and growling.

Suddenly, there was a nose nudging at her arm. Zoe risked a peek. A familiar face was staring up at her.

"Jossy!" she said, clasping the trembling cub tightly and curling around him. "I've got you. You're all right now."

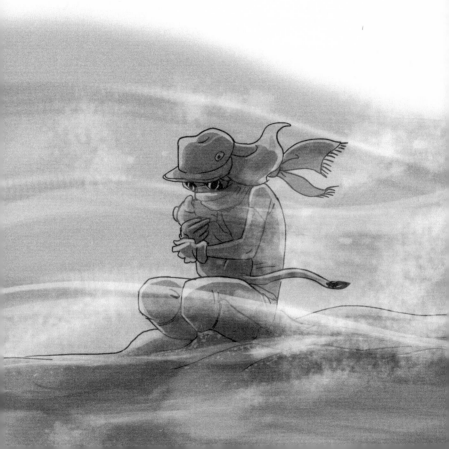

The lion cub seemed to sense that he had reached safety. He lay in Zoe's arms, sneezing and shaking his head to free himself of the fine sand that covered his snout.

Zoe wished she could contact Ben on her BUG and tell him she'd found Jossy, but all Zoe could do now was to wait until the storm moved on. And she had no idea how long that would be.

* * *

Ben lay under his shelter, fighting the urge to race to Zoe's rescue. He admired her courage for going after Jossy, but she'd taken their mission too far. The sound of the sand beating on his shelter was deafening. As the wind whipped around, it caught the corners of the sail, making it hard to keep the shelter stable.

Ben could feel the sand beginning to cover him. First his feet, then his back. He kept shaking it off, horrified at the thought of being buried alive.

After what felt like an eternity, the sound of the storm began to die away. Ben cautiously raised a corner of the sail and looked out. Zoe was nowhere to be seen, and neither was Jossy. The air grew still. The blown sand was banked up in smooth slopes and mounds against trees and around bushes and rocks.

A terrible thought came to him. Was Zoe somewhere under there, struggling to breathe?

Ben jumped when he heard a shout close behind him. He leaped to his feet, threw the sail aside and turned. Just a few paces away was a shallow bank of sand.

Zoe was emerging from the far side with Jossy in her arms! Ben gave a shout of relief, ripped off his goggles and cotton scarf, and ran toward his sister.

"That was scary!" called Zoe, uncovering her face. "If only I'd known I was so close. But I did find our naughty little friend!"

"I'm not sure who was the naughty one," said Ben sternly. "You should never have left the shelter in a storm like that."

"I know," admitted Zoe. "But if I hadn't, we might have lost Jossy for good."

Ben grinned. "And you say I'm the one who takes all the risks!" he said.

Jossy wriggled in Zoe's arms. "Okay, boy," she said soothingly. "We're going now."

Ben reached out and stroked the cub to help calm him. Then he looked up at the sky. Over in the west, the sun was beginning to sink toward the dunes. "We won't get much farther before nightfall," he said. "We should set up camp for now, and head for the pool in the morning."

"Good idea," Zoe said. She wiped her mouth with her hand. "And I need some water! I'm really dried out after that storm. I bet Jossy would like a drink, too."

Ben held up the water bottle and shook it. "Not much left," he said. He saw the look of alarm on Zoe's face. "Don't worry, we'll think of something. There are a few plants growing here, so there must be water somewhere."

"I just remembered something I saw on TV," said Zoe. "A program about the people of the Kalahari. They dug up melons and drank the fluid inside. The melons had leaves that looked like dandelions and were on long stalks under the surface."

"Then let's get digging," said Ben.

Jossy seemed sleepy again, so they made him comfortable in the backpack and began their search. There were clumps of yellow spiky grass and thorn bushes pushing up through the newly laid sand, but no sign of the dandelion-like leaves.

The sun was very low now, and sinking fast. Zoe began to scrape away the sand, trying to ignore the overwhelming dryness in her mouth.

They searched and dug until darkness fell, but they didn't find anything.

"Time to stop," said Ben, running his tongue over his dry lips. "We're not getting anywhere. The sandstorm hid any melon leaves. We should get some sleep."

"Agreed," said Zoe. "I'm even thirstier now."

Ben handed her their water bottle. "There's about three sips each, so make the most of it!" he said.

Zoe felt the drops of warm water disappear in her dry mouth. She took out Jossy's milk. The little lion cub looked at her drowsily as she gently pushed the teat between his teeth. He began to suck. Before long, the bottle was empty.

"He's drank it all!" she said in alarm. "There's nothing left. What are we going to do?"

"Don't worry," Ben said. "I've got an idea." He pulled the sail across the sand and draped it over a couple of nearby bushes, letting it dip in the middle. "We'll sleep under here, and we'll find water in that hollow when we wake up."

"I'm not falling for that one, Ben," said Zoe, smirking. "It's not going to rain tonight."

"But there will be condensation," said
Ben. "The moisture in the air will condense
on the sail and run down into the hollow."

Ben heaved the backpacks under the
shelter, crawled in, and pulled out an
energy bar. "At least we have a little food
left," he said.

It was hard to eat the energy bar
without a drink. It stuck to the roofs of their
mouths. Their lips cracked open as they
chewed.

Zoe wrapped up the rest of the bar and put it away. Ben wasn't doing much better. He took up his BUG. "It's working now that the storm passed," he said, tapping at the buttons. "I just texted Erika that we'll be near the pool in the morning. She said to contact her again then."

Zoe looked down at the little lion cub. His head was on his paws and his eyes were closed. "I'll check on your mother," she told him, "and see how far she's gotten."

But when the signal appeared on her screen, Zoe's face fell. "She still hasn't moved, Ben." She gulped hard. "What if I killed her?"

CHAPTER 9

DESERT DREAMS

"I'm sure the lioness is fine," said Ben, putting his arm around his sister. "She probably woke up just after we left and has made her way back to the pride."

"Then why is her signal still in the same place?" Zoe said, trying to hold back tears. "I gave her too much tranquilizer. I should've known better. She'll be at risk from predators now — and that other lion."

Ben gave her a friendly nudge. "It's probably your BUG getting it wrong," he said. "It might still be malfunctioning."

Zoe managed a half-hearted smile. "That could be it," she said. "I'm being silly, sorry."

She went silent as they heard strange wailing sounds fill the air around them. "What's that?" she said, clutching Ben's arm. She peered out over the sand. It was dark now. She felt herself shiver. "It's so creepy, like spooky musical instruments."

"Ghosts of the Kalahari!" said Ben, his eyes wide.

"Don't be silly," said Zoe. "It can't be." She paused. "Can it?"

Ben grinned. "Perhaps they're phantoms of travelers lost in the desert," he said in a sinister voice. "Searching for their next victims."

Zoe rolled her eyes.

"Or maybe it's a bunch of camels playing clarinets?" Ben said.

Zoe punched Ben in the shoulder. "You know what it really is, don't you?" she said.

Ben grinned at her. "It's the sand singing!" he said. "I read about it on the plane. It happens here in the desert when the wind has dropped."

Zoe punched her brother's arm. "How can the sand make that noise?" she asked.

"The wind drives the sand up the dunes," Ben said. "But in the end, the top gets too heavy and starts to slide. That's what we can hear."

"Weird!" said Zoe. "You wouldn't expect it to sound so eerie." She shivered and moved closer to her brother. "The temperature's dropping."

She looked out from under the shelter up at the black sky. It was filled with bright stars. "It's going to be a cold night."

Ben checked the little cub's leg wound by under a flashlight's beam. "His leg looks clean," he said. "Let's get some sleep."

He unfolded their sleeping bags and they curled up as close to each other as they could.

"Jossy makes a nice heating pad," Zoe said as the little cub lay beside her.

In the distance, she could hear cries of nocturnal creatures calling to each other. She made sure that the scent disperser was still working on her BUG and then analyzed the calls.

"Jackals," she told Ben. "Leopard and hyenas, too! It's predator city out there."

"This could be a problem," said Ben. "They won't smell us, but they might catch Jossy's scent. We need a deterrent."

"One of us stays awake with the tranquilizer gun?" said Zoe.

"No need!" said Ben. He tapped some keys on his BUG and aimed a hologram image of a crackling fire just beyond their shelter. "That should keep them away."

Jossy suddenly wriggled and scratched his ear. He looked around, interested in the distant calls.

"Better make sure he doesn't wander off again," said Zoe. She took the rope from Ben's backpack and fastened it round Jossy's body in a harness, tying the other end firmly to her wrist. "Now if you make a break for it, you'll be dragging me with you!"

Zoe stroked the cub's back as he rubbed his cheek against her face. "He's such a darling," she said. "I wish I could keep him." She caught sight of her brother rolling his eyes. "I know, I can't." She grinned.

Jossy snuggled down and was soon breathing deeply, his paws twitching as he dreamed. Zoe huddled close to the warm cub. The air on her face was getting very cold. She began to wish that the hologram image of the fire was real.

A while later, Zoe pulled her sleeping bag around her ears. Ben was already asleep, but Zoe couldn't get comfortable. The creepy song of the sands was still echoing in the distance, and that got her worrying about the lioness again.

Zoe was sure that she had used the correct amount of tranquilizer. Then why hadn't the signal moved?

As her anxious thoughts whirled around her head, Zoe felt like she'd never fall asleep.

The next thing she knew, Zoe found herself at the top of a sand dune ready to toboggan down toward a huge pool of cool, inviting water. She jumped on her sled and was about to launch herself down when Grandma appeared, grabbed her wrist, and tugged it hard.

Zoe jerked awake. The sky outside their shelter was dashed with orange and purple like it was on fire. She peered at it, puzzled.

"It's dawn!" she said. She'd been dreaming. Of course Grandma wasn't here with them. Also, she was thirstier than she'd ever felt in her life.

But something was pulling at her wrist. She hadn't been dreaming that. She sat up and looked around her. It was Jossy tugging at his leash! The little cub was scampering about at her feet, limping slightly.

The cub nosed the ground, while pawing at a small, dark object.

"You're feeling better, Jossy," said Zoe. "That looks like playing to me."

Zoe gave Ben a nudge. He stirred and gazed blankly at her, his hair sticking up. "What's going on?" Ben muttered, rubbing his eyes.

"Our patient has recovered," Zoe said. "He's playing a game."

Ben focused on the cub. "What's he playing with?" he asked as Jossy pounced again.

With dread, Zoe realized what it was. "It's a scorpion!" she cried. "And it's about to strike!"

CHAPTER 10

PREDATOR AND PREY

Zoe yanked at Jossy's rope, dragging him toward her, but the angry scorpion darted after him. Ben was out of his sleeping bag in a flash. He crouched down, fumbling with one hand for his hat.

"I'll trap it," he said. But he couldn't seem to find his hat. He didn't dare take his eyes off the scorpion. It had stopped, tail twitching, within reach of Jossy. At last, Ben's fingers closed on the brim of his cap. He snatched it up and slammed it over the scorpion.

ZIP! The sting poked through the fabric.

"Wow!" Ben said as he whipped his hand away just in time. "That was close!"

He flipped the cap over, catching the scorpion inside. Then he swung it like a racket and sent the poisonous insect flying far away from their camp.

"Where are some meerkats when you need them," he said. "They're immune to the stings, and they'd eat them."

Zoe shuddered. "Yeah," she said. She was finding it hard to speak because her mouth was so dry.

Ben was panting from his exertions. "I shouldn't be feeling like this," he said. "I'm getting dehydrated."

The sun was now peeking over the distant dunes.

Ben crawled out from their cover to inspect the roof of their shelter. "Look at this," he said. "It worked!"

Ben and Zoe each scooped up a handful of the cold water that was caught in the dip of the sail and gulped the liquid down.

"No more!" said Ben. "We have to save the rest for later."

Ben held the sail carefully while Zoe collected every drop in their bottles.

Zoe used some water to make Jossy a little of his special milk, then stuffed the bottles in Ben's backpack.

"We'd better get moving," said Ben. He turned off the fire hologram and pulled his backpack toward him. A trailing strap attracted Jossy's attention and he pounced on it with a small growl. Grasping it in his front paws, he bit at it. Then he jumped to his feet and scampered around in circles.

"That's a good sign," said Zoe. "He doesn't seem to be in any pain from that wound, and it looks like it's healing well."

Ben grinned at the little cub's antics. It hurt his cracked lips, but he was happy that Jossy was feeling better. "We'll have to keep him on his leash or he'll run all over the place. He's certainly not going to let us put him in a backpack now."

Zoe grabbed the rope. "Here, Jossy!" she said. She dangled the end in front of him and he swiped at it. "I might have to play with him like this the whole way," Zoe said.

Ben brought up a map on his BUG. "The pool is to the west," he said. "It shouldn't take more than an hour."

"What about his mom's signal?" asked Zoe. She brought up the tracking screen. "Oh no, she's still at the well." Zoe tested the BUG's other functions just to be sure it was working. It was.

Ben squeezed her arm. "We'll get Erika to take us back there after we've delivered Jossy," he said. He navigated through the menu. "I'm setting my BUG to pick up lion calls. Then we'll know that we're taking our little cub to the right place."

Zoe pulled firmly on the leash. "Come on, Jossy," she said. "Let's get you home."

They packed up and set out across the flat, baked earth, allowing themselves occasional sips of water from their small supply. The dunes were behind them now. Shading his eyes, Ben could see a herd of wildebeest bunched around a small patch of green in the distance. The sky was a deep turquoise with tiny white clouds. And it was very hot. Ben felt his head swimming, but he knew he had to keep going.

Jossy scampered along, pulling at the lead and sniffing at every plant and rock.

"Not long now, Jossy," said Zoe. "Has the BUG picked up any lion cries?"

Ben shook his head. "Nothing on the screen yet," he said. "But that doesn't mean they're not nearby. They could be asleep."

Ben and Zoe reached the bottom of a stony ridge. At that moment, they heard a scraping noise, and a shower of pebbles came rolling down toward them. They looked up to see a large antelope standing proudly at the top. "It's a gemsbok," Ben whispered.

"What a beautiful creature," Zoe said.

Then Jossy saw the gemsbok. He let out an excited mew and tried to scramble toward the ridge.

With a scuffle of hooves, the creature disappeared. "I think our little cub's hungry," said Ben. "He wants to do some hunting. He really is feeling better. Let's get to the top of this ridge and check out the view. We might spot the pride."

"We have to be careful," said Zoe. "We don't want them spotting us first."

They crept up to the top of the ridge and scanned the terrain ahead. The gemsbok was bounding down toward his herd. They were grazing under a baobab tree. Beyond the tree, a group of buffalo wandered across the grassy sand.

"There's the pool!" said Ben, pointing at a circle of trees in the distance. It was bright green against the orange land. "Over to the west."

Zoe bent down and scratched Jossy between the ears. "Nearly home," she said. "At least I hope so. I can't see any lions."

Ben checked his BUG. "It's picking up lion cries now," he said. "And they're definitely coming from those trees. I think we've found Jossy's family."

They headed down the ridge. Something was lying on the ground ahead. "It's a dead gemsbok," said Ben as they came closer to it. "Predators have been here. I bet it was the lions, too."

Jossy sniffed the air eagerly and pulled hard at the rope. "He's hungry," said Zoe. "Is he old enough to eat meat?"

"He seems to be," said Ben. "Let him try."

Whatever had killed the gemsbok had fed well, but there was still some meat left.

Jossy pulled Zoe over and began to eat hungrily. "He's going to be okay," said Zoe.

A low chuckling sound behind her made her spin around. "Ben!" she said quickly. "We've got trouble."

Ben turned and froze. Several bristling hyenas were slinking menacingly toward them with their heads and ears high.

The ridges of spotted hair on their backs were stiff, meaning they were being aggressive. The leader made a growling chuckle in its throat as they began to circle Ben, Zoe, and Jossy.

"I think this gemsbok was going to be their breakfast," said Zoe.

"Not anymore," Ben whispered back. "The way they're looking at us, I think we're on the menu now."

Jossy stopped eating and edged away from the snarling pack. The hyenas watched Jossy, tendrils of drool hanging from their lips.

Ben used the distraction to slowly lift his tranquilizer gun. "There's no way I can shoot them all," he whispered, lowering his arm. "We need to try something else. We have to be more aggressive than them."

Ben took a deep breath and waved his arms wildly, making loud growling noises. Then he stamped toward the pack, slamming his feet into the sand.

Zoe joined in. The hyenas stopped their advance and eyed them warily.

"It's not enough," said Ben. "I'm going to try something else."

He grabbed his BUG and was searching for the setting to make it roar like a lion when a deep-throated growl boomed out all around them.

The leader of the pack gave a high-pitched yowl and the hyenas immediately scattered, bounding away across the desert.

Ben looked at Zoe in amazement. "Was that your BUG?" he asked. "It certainly did the trick. Nice work."

Zoe was gazing over Ben's shoulder. He saw her eyes flicker with fear. "It wasn't me," she whispered. She pointed up at the ridge. Ben turned around slowly.

A huge lion with a magnificent mane was standing at the top of the ridge. It lifted its head and gave another tremendous roar.

Ben and Zoe dived for cover behind a rock, dragging Jossy with them.

The lion stalked slowly toward their hiding place, growling deeply. Jossy began to mew loudly.

"Shh!" said Zoe. "You'll give us away!" With a trembling hand, she slowly stroked Jossy's head in an effort to calm him. But the little cub mewed louder, wriggling to break free from the harness.

The lion stopped in his tracks. His ears twitched as he tried to track the sound. Then his gaze fell on the rock. Slowly and purposefully, he padded toward it.

Suddenly, Jossy wriggled out of his harness and broke away from Zoe's hold. The cub bounded toward the lion, giving little growls as he went.

Ben fumbled with his gun, his fingers sliding around the trigger. "I think he's trying to protect us," he said in horror.

"Come back!" called Zoe. "You're too small, Jossy. You don't stand a chance."

But Jossy scampered between the lion's legs and began playfully biting his tail!

Then he rolled over on his back and batted it. The huge creature looked down at him.

Ben edged around the rock. He got a firm grip on the gun, raised it, and took aim.

Zoe caught his arm. "Wait!" she cried.

Instead of attacking the little cub, the huge lion gave him a friendly cuff with his paw. Ben lowered the gun and grinned. "There's only one male lion who would accept that kind of behavior from Jossy," he said. "It must be his dad! And from the deep color of his mane, I'd say he's the dominant male of the pride."

"Then it must be Jossy's pride at the pool," said Zoe. "I hope the mom's there." She looked at the tracking screen on her BUG. The orange light was still at the well. "She still hasn't moved," Zoe whispered. "I'm really worried about her, Ben."

"I'm sure she's fine," said Ben, trying to sound confident. But he could see that Zoe didn't look convinced. "Look!" he said.

The male lion turned and strode toward the distant trees around the pool.

Jossy trotted along at his side, nipping at his leg until his father butted him off. The little cub went rolling across the red earth, jumped to his feet, and scampered back to his father's side.

"Let's follow them," said Ben. "We have to report that he's safely back with the pride."

"Who's going to look after him if his mom isn't there?" asked Zoe.

"I don't think that'll be a problem," said Ben. "All the females help each other to rear their cubs. They're like aunts."

Keeping their distance, they followed the lions toward the pool. When they reached the trees, they stayed just out of sight. "Wow!" whispered Zoe.

The pool was as big as a football field. It was surrounded on all sides by palm trees, baobabs, and camel's thorns with their ferny leaves. Water glinted in the harsh sunlight as it rippled near the banks. Grass and small flowers grew under the trees. The air was full of bird cries and songs.

Ben pointed over to the far side. Stretched out on a sandbank was a group of lions. Some were asleep and others were crouched and drinking at the water's edge. Several young cubs were playing together in the shade.

"I count fifteen of them," whispered Ben. "That's not a bad size for a pride of lions."

Jossy and his dad walked over to the group. At once, a lioness sprang up. "Is that his mom?" whispered Zoe.

"If it is, he'll go straight to her," said Ben.

Now other lionesses were on their feet, all nosing around the baby. But Jossy trotted from one to the other as if searching for his mother.

"She's not there," said Zoe, close to tears. "And it's all my fault."

CHAPTER 11

A PURRFECT REUNION

Jossy finally flopped down next to a scrawny old lioness. She sniffed him suspiciously.

"Do you think he smells strange to her?" asked Zoe. "He's been away from the pride for a while. I hope he doesn't get rejected."

"No way," said Ben. Just then, the female gave Jossy a thorough licking. He leaned against her as she flattened his ears and pushed him this way and that.

Once the cleaning was finished, Jossy jumped up and began to search amongst the females again.

"We brought him home, but his mom's not here," said Zoe. Her eyes began to well with tears.

Ben put his arm around Zoe. "It's not your fault," he said. "Besides, the other females are taking care of Jossy. He'll be fine."

Ben took his BUG, put it on speaker, and hit the call key for Erika. "Hello there," came her voice. "How's the mission going?"

"The cub's back with the pride —" Ben began to say.

"But we don't know where his mother is," Zoe said. "I had to tranquilize her . . ." Zoe broke into a sob.

Ben hugged his sister and told Erika everything that had happened.

"Your uncle will be proud of you," said Erika. "And Zoe, try not to worry. You did everything you could for the lioness."

"The moment you pick us up, can you bring us to the well so we can see what's happened to the lioness?" asked Zoe.

"Of course," said Erika. "I'll land as close to you as I can. On the WASP, it won't take you very long to get to the plane. I'll send you the coordinates. And I've got plenty of water, so you'll be feeling better in no time."

"Oh, um, about the WASP," said Ben. "Erika, we had a little accident." He told her about the encounter with the hungry lion.

"Then I'll arrange for someone to come pick you up," said Erika. "See you soon!"

* * *

They sat in the shelter of the trees and watched as Jossy finally settled down next to the female who had washed him. She fed him, but Jossy kept stopping to look around for his real mom. The other cubs wrestled with each other while the adults stretched out lazily in the heat.

Ben and Zoe sipped at their remaining water and ate energy bars. It was getting very hot. Zoe felt her eyelids begin to droop. Suddenly her BUG vibrated.

"I'm here, just due south of you," came Erika's voice. "I'm safely upwind of the lions, so we shouldn't have any problems making it to you without alerting the pride."

"Why would she worry about the lions picking up her scent?" asked Ben. "She's got a scent disperser, doesn't she?"

Zoe shaded her eyes and peered out over the horizon. "It's not herself she's worried about," she said, pointing into the distance. "It's our transportation!"

Ben followed her finger and let out a groan. "Great," he said. "More camels!"

"We're on our way," Zoe told Erika. "Over and out." Zoe tried to act normal, but inside she felt miserable. She couldn't escape the horrible thought that she had accidentally killed Jossy's mom.

At that moment, a high-pitched mewing drew their attention back to the pride. Jossy had left the group, yowling excitedly as he ran toward something approaching in the distance.

The other lions stood up and stared.
"It's a lioness," whispered Ben.

The newcomer was limping slowly
toward the water. She had scratches on
her side and her muzzle was bleeding. She
stopped when she saw Jossy and made
a deep rumbling noise at the cub. For a
moment, none of them moved.

Jossy threw himself at her, running between her legs and pawing at her sides. The lioness slumped to the ground and Jossy crept between her front paws, nudging her face with his.

"It's his mom!" Zoe cried out in delight.

"She looks like she's been in a fight," said Ben. "I wonder if she crossed paths with the same lone lion we did. It would explain why she's taken so long to get here."

"Or the hyenas," Zoe said. "I'm just glad she made it back."

Ben and Zoe watched the scene of the reunion. Jossy climbed happily all over his weary mother, kneading at her with his claws like a kitten. She nuzzled him and rubbed her cheeks against his.

The other lionesses padded around them, sniffing and licking at her wounds. Zoe's eyes were shining as she watched the pride settle down. The little cub curled up contentedly next to his mom.

Zoe turned to Ben. "Why didn't her tracking dart show on the BUG?" she asked.

Ben checked the BUG screen and showed his sister. "It is showing," Ben said with a grin. "You must have missed your shot and tracked the well, doofus!"

Zoe smirked at her brother. "I may have missed the mark," she admitted, "but at least I didn't trash our ride."

"Fair enough," Ben said. Then he jumped to his feet and tugged at Zoe's arm. "Time to go. Erika's waiting."

"Do we have to?" asked Zoe. "I could watch these lions forever."

"And miss the chance of seeing me fall off another camel?" asked Ben.

"Ha, I'd never miss that!" Zoe said. She got to her feet and took one last look back. "Bye, Jossy. I'm so glad you're home safe."

Then the twins crept away quietly through the trees.

* * *

As they approached Erika, Ben's BUG vibrated. "It's a call from WILD," he said.

"Greetings!" came their uncle's cheerful voice. "Erika's brought me up to speed. Well done, you two!"

"There's more," Zoe said happily. "Jossy's mom made it back after all!"

"Well then!" their uncle boomed. "It's another perfect end to a perfect mission for Zoe and Ben!"

Ben glanced ahead to where one of the camels was snorting and stamping its hoof.

"That one's yours," Erika said, pointing at the angry camel.

"Almost perfect," Ben said with a laugh.

THE AUTHORS

Jan Burchett and **Sara Vogler** were already friends when they discovered they both wanted to write children's books, and that it was much more fun to do it together. They have since written over a hundred and thirty stories ranging from educational books and stories for younger readers to young adult fiction. They have written for series such as Dinosaur Cove and Beast Quest, and they are authors of the Gargoylz books.

THE ILLUSTRATOR

Diane Le Feyer discovered a passion for drawing and animation at the age of five. In 2002, she graduated with honors from the Ecole Emile Cohl school of design. Diane worked as a character designer, 3D modeler, and animator in the video games industry before joining the Cartoon Saloon animation studio, where she worked as a director, animator, illustrator, and character designer. Diane was also a part of the early design and development of the movie *The Secret of Kells*.

GLOSSARY

accelerated (ak-SEL-uh-rate-id)—moved faster and faster

anxiously (ANGK-shuhss-lee)—eagerly or impatiently

dominant (DOM-uh-nuhnt)—most influential or powerful. The dominant male in a pride of lions is the pride's leader.

hologram (HOL-uh-gram)—an image made by laser beams that looks real and three-dimensional

hyena (hye-EE-nuh)—a wild animal that looks somewhat like a dog. It eats meat and has a shrieking howl.

mane (MAYN)—the long, thick hair on the head and neck of a male lion or horse

pride (PRIDE)—a pack of lions

sandstorm (SAND-storm)—a windstorm in the desert that sends gusts of sand through the air at high speeds

stalked (STAWKD)—hunted or tracked a person or an animal in a quiet, secretive way

AFRICAN LION
STATUS: VULNERABLE

Lions are found mainly in the sub-Saharan region of Africa. They live in savannahs, grasslands, dense bush, and woodlands. Over the last thirty years, Africa has lost almost 70 percent of its lion population due to:

PREDATORS: Lions have no natural predators. Humans are the biggest threat to their survival. As the human population around national parks increases, so does contact with lions, increasing the chance that lions will be harmed or killed.

LOSS OF HABITAT: People are taking over lion territory, which causes conflicts between lions and humans.

POISONING: Livestock owners sometimes poison or shoot lions that kill their cattle.

POACHERS: The lion is one of the most prized "trophy kills" by hunters.

BUT IT'S NOT ALL BAD FOR THE AFRICAN LION! Many lions live in protected national parks. Conservations groups are working hard to preserve the numbers of lions. For instance, the African Wildlife Foundation has lion conservation research projects in Tanzania and Botswana.

DISCUSSION QUESTIONS

1. Ben and Zoe are passionate about saving animals. What are you passionate about? Talk about things you love doing.

2. The twins love animals. What's your favorite animal species? Do you have any pets? Discuss animals.

3. What are some everyday things that you can do to help the environment? Discuss ways you can make your community a better place.

WRITING PROMPTS

1. Zoe and Ben get to use lots of differeng gadgets in their animal-saving adventures. Design your own gadget. What does your invention do? Write about it, then draw a picture of your gadget.

2. A scary sandstorm wreaks havoc with Ben and Zoe's rescue attempt. What's the scariest thing that you've experienced? What happened? Write about it.

3. Ben and Zoe travel by go-kart, WASP, airplane, camel, and a variety of other forms of transportation. What kind of traveling have you done? Where did you go? How did you get there? Write about your travels.